My Tiny
TREASURY
Of Stories And Rhymes

This paperback edition published in 2006 by
STRATHEARN BOOKS LIMITED
Toronto, Canada

3 5 7 9 10 8 6 4 2

ISBN 1-89546-469-2

Published in 1998 in a hardback format
Originally published by Bookmart Limited as
The Teddy Bear Collection,
Fairy Tales from the Brothers Grimm,
Fairy Tales from Hans Christian Andersen,
and *The Children's Classic Poetry Collection.*

Produced for Bookmart Limited by Nicola Baxter
PO Box 71, Diss, Norfolk IP22 2DT
Editorial consultant: Ronne Randall
Designer: Amanda Hawkes

Printed in Thailand

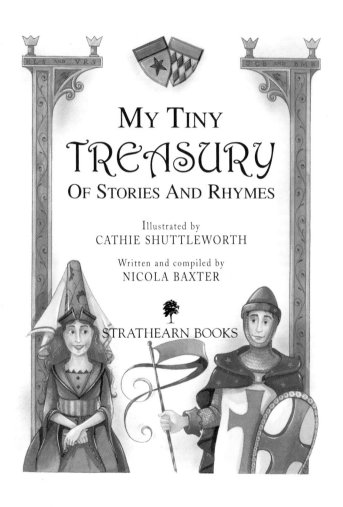

My Tiny
TREASURY
Of Stories And Rhymes

Illustrated by
CATHIE SHUTTLEWORTH

Written and compiled by
NICOLA BAXTER

STRATHEARN BOOKS

CONTENTS

Teddy Bear Tales
The Teddy Bears' Picnic 8
A Bear With Bells 18
The Little Lost Bears 28
The Ghostly Bear 38
The Bear Who Was Bare 52
The Littlest Bear 62
The Real Teddy Bear 64
The Buzzing Bear 72
The Adventurous Bear 78
Bears Everywhere 84
The Bears Who Were Brave 90
The Bear Who Couldn't Stay Awake 94

Fairy Tales

Hansel and Gretel 100
The Little Mermaid 106
Sleeping Beauty 116
Thumbelina 122
The Frog Prince 130
The Emperor's New Clothes 136
The Fisherman and His Wife 144
The Princess and the Pea 150
The Elves and the Shoemaker 158
The Snow Queen 164
The Musicians of Bremen 180
The Emperor and the
Nightingale 186
Little Red Riding Hood 196
The Ugly Duckling 202
Snow White and the Seven
Dwarfs 210
The Shadow 220
The Tinderbox 226
Rapunzel 230
The Fir Tree 238
The Twelve Dancing
Princesses 242
The Brave Tin Soldier 252

TEDDY
BEAR
TALES

The Real Story of

THE TEDDY BEARS' PICNIC

Colonel Augustus Bearington (retired) here! The time has come to set the record straight about the illustrious event known as the Teddy Bears' Picnic. I was only a young bear at the time, but I remember it so well. Throw another log on the fire, Mungo. My threadbare old ears feel the cold.

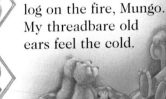

First of all, you must remember
that things were different in those
days. Bears were less common then,
and only very lucky children lived with
a bear of their own. Today you young
bears live in homes that may have
four or five bears. You have company.

Children who shared their homes with bears usually spent most of their time in the nursery with a woman called a nanny. She looked after the children while their mother and father were busy—a job that any self-respecting bear could do in his sleep.

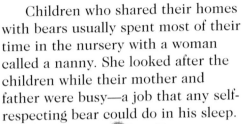

Children had to be seen and not heard in those days, and nannies got very cross indeed if they didn't wash behind their ears.

In those days, bears were not able to meet very often. The best chance was in the afternoon, when nannies took their charges to the park. Then children would play with friends from other big houses, nannies would chat and knit with other nannies, and bears, of course, could have a word with other bears. It was a part of the day that every bear looked forward to.

I think it was Rufus who first put the idea into our heads. Rufus was a reddish-brown bear from a rather well-to-do home. The little girl he lived with was a Lady. Yes, a real Lady, whose mother was a Duchess. But Rufus was a friendly bear, who never put on airs.

One day, Rufus told us that the Duchess was giving a special party for Very Important People. The Queen herself would be coming!

"You know, Gussie," said Rufus, "we bears should have a party of our own. We could invite all the Most Important Bears in town."

Well, the idea caught on at once. Every bear for miles around heard of the plan, and we soon had a guest list of over a hundred. But could we find a place big enough for the party?

Rufus didn't hesitate for a moment. "We'll hold it right here," he said.

It was obvious! I was a muttonhead not to have thought of it myself. After that, there was no time to lose. I was in charge, of course. It takes a military mind to organize an event on that scale. And I also came up with the date for the picnic.

Luckily, several young bears helped with the preparations. You'd be amazed what can be smuggled among a baby's blankets. And we did not forget cushions for the old bears.

At last the great day arrived. It was the day of the Queen's Jubilee. She had been on the throne for umpteen years, and her subjects lined the streets to cheer.

Meanwhile, dozens of bears padded along the back streets to the park.

What an afternoon that was! I met my dear Rosa—but that's another story.

What was that you said, Mungo?
Yes, someone did see us.
I don't know who it was.
Yes, there was a song.
It was quite popular,
although the facts
were quite wrong,
of course. We were
nowhere near the
woods. All make
believe? Just you
look here. I've carried
this worn photograph in
my pocket for over sixty years.

Stir the fire up, Mungo. The
smoke's getting in my eyes. Whose
turn is it next for a story?

The Amazing Story of

A Bear With Bells

Thank you, Colonel. I'm new to your circle, so let me introduce myself. I'm Hermann P. Bear from Switzerland. Now, with all respect, I've found that today's bears are just as brave and clever as the noble bears of yesterday. My story proves just that.

The story is about a friend of mine, back home among the mountains. I'll call him Fritz. He is a modest bear and, if he ever appears in public again, he would not want the world to know the part he played in the Great Zurich Bank Robbery.

Now Fritz is a jolly bear, but since the day he was sewn, he has suffered a great hardship. Around his neck, his toymaker put a collar of tiny bells. I can see you are horrified. Yes, poor Fritz could not move without jingling. He had to sit still, hour after hour, for fear of revealing our great secret.

Now Fritz was such an unusual
bear that he was bought by a collector.
Yes, a grown-up person who had over
a hundred very beautiful bears. The
grown-up was a rich man, who cared
more about our value in money than
the very fine bears we all were.

One day, this gentleman went to
America to buy some more bears. While
he was gone, he put all his dearest
possessions in the bank, and that
included some of us bears. We were
kept in a trunk in a large safe-deposit
box, where a bear only had to move a
whisker to set off alarms and sirens.

We had been in the bank for two
long weeks, when the Great Robbery
took place. We heard an explosion
and felt ourselves being jiggled about
as the trunk was carried out, but we
couldn't see much through the keyhole.

It was some hours later, in a cold Swiss dawn, that the robbers arrived at their hideaway—a cave tucked away in the side of a mountain. They hid their truck and set about dividing up their ill-gotten gains.

All went well as they opened the boxes of gold coins and jewels, but when they saw us, they were very angry indeed. I'm afraid that the language of the unpleasant man who looked down at us was quite unrepeatable. My ears turned pink, I can tell you.

The stupid man had no idea we were valuable bears at all. He kicked the trunk so hard it toppled over, and we fell onto the cold floor of the cave, with icicles dripping down on us. My fur has never been the same since.

It was almost dark when we heard noises outside. It was the police! But the cave was well hidden.

All the robbers had to do was keep still. As you know, humans cannot hear bear speech, so we were powerless to make a noise, but Fritz was a very brave bear. He jumped to his feet and began to jingle and jangle as hard as he could. In the silence, it seemed to be an enormous noise. The most vicious-looking of the robbers leaped toward Fritz with a terrible cry. Just then, a powerful flash- light lit the dramatic scene.

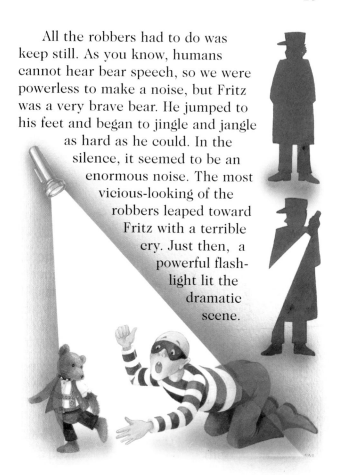

Well, the rest is history. The robbers were caught, the loot was recovered, and we bears were taken into custody as evidence. Eventually, we were sold to new owners, all over the world.

And Fritz? Well, I cannot be sure. He fell behind a boulder and was not discovered with the rest of us. There are sometimes stories of a strange jingling sound to be heard in the mountains. I hope that Fritz is happy, living the life of a free and furry bear.

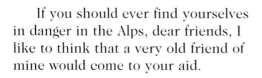

If you should ever find yourselves in danger in the Alps, dear friends, I like to think that a very old friend of mine would come to your aid.

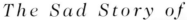

The Sad Story of

THE LITTLE LOST BEARS

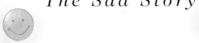

The story of Fritz has made me think of an important subject. I am speaking, of course, of lost bears. I've never forgotten what my mother said to me: "Belinda Bear, always stay close to your owner, especially on trains, for there are many bears today sitting in Lost Property Offices."

Well, when I was a little bear, I did
not always listen to my mother as
well as I should. My friend Bessie and
I got into all kinds of trouble. We spent
more time in the bathtub than
any bear would wish,
having jelly, or paint, or
honey washed out of
our fur. But although
we were often in
disgrace, we were
always careful not to
get lost. The idea
of the Lost Property
Office was *too*
horrible. We made
sure that the little girl
who looked after us
never left us behind.

One day, Maisie (that was the little girl's name) went to visit her grandmother. And she went by train!

"Let's hold paws," said Bessie. "Then, if we get lost, we'll be together."

So Bessie and I went with Maisie on the train, and I can tell you that trains are *not* safe places for bears. First a lady squashed my ear with her shopping bag.

Then another lady with a little dog sat down nearby. The dog seized hold of Bessie's leg and tried to pull her under the seat!

Of course, we expect humans to be silly. They don't have a bear's sharp brain. But it was the train itself that caused our biggest problem. With every jiggle and jounce, it jolted us nearer to the edge of the seat.

It was sure to happen. As the
train rumbled around a corner, we
tumbled onto the floor and rolled
under the table.

"We'll be left behind," I moaned.
"It's the Lost Property Office for us."

But Bessie had one of her Good
Ideas. I listened carefully.

"If we climb inside Maisie's bag,"
she said, "we can't be left behind."

It *did* seem to be a good idea. We
climbed into the bag and fell fast
asleep at once.

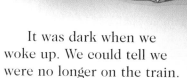

It was dark when we
woke up. We could tell we
were no longer on the train.

"We must be in Maisie's
grandmother's house,"
Bessie whispered.

We soon heard footsteps.
The bag opened and a face
looked down at us. It was
the first lady from the train!

I don't know which of us was more surprised.

"Look!" she called to her husband. "These bears belonged to the little girl on the train. What can I do with them?"

It was then we heard the words we had been dreading.

"Take them to the Lost Property Office," said the man.

"We'll have to escape," said Bessie.

"Is that one of your Good Ideas?" I asked, but I knew that Bessie was right.

Late that night, we crawled out of a downstairs window and set off for home.

When morning came, we were deep in a forest. Paw in paw, we wandered through the trees.

Day after day, we walked on sore paws. We ate berries and slept among the mossy roots of the trees. Once a bad bird tried to peck out our fur to line its nest. Once I fell into a hole in a tree and only just managed to climb out. At night, we often cried ourselves to sleep.

One afternoon, we were found by
a family taking a walk. The little girl
brought me here to join you all and
gave Bessie to her cousin. From that
day to this, I have never seen Bessie
or Maisie, and my furry face is often
wet with tears. If there were human
children listening to me now, I would
tell them to cuddle their bears and
keep them safe. I hope Maisie has
found a new bear to make her happy.

The Scary Story of

THE GHOSTLY BEAR

Little bears, the story I am about to tell you is very, very scary. If you get frightened, you must put your paws over your ears and cuddle up to a grown-up bear. My aunty told me this story when I was a very little bear.

Once upon a time, in a faraway land, there was a huge castle. The castle stood empty for many years, but one day there was great excitement in the nearby village. The owner of the castle was coming to visit. Now no one had ever seen this mysterious owner, so there was a lot of talk about who it might be.

"I've heard it is a Countess," said the baker. "A witch put a curse on her. Now she wears a veil to hide her ugly face."

"No," replied the blacksmith, "the owner *is* a witch. She travels at night, and has a black cat."

"Nonsense!" The schoolteacher waved her stick. "It is simply an old lady who cannot move around very well."

Every day, the children in the village looked out for the important visitor, but no one came. Then, one morning, a little girl called Lucy noticed smoke rising above the highest tower in the castle.

"She must have come in the night!" she cried. "She must be a witch after all."

When they heard this, the villagers were very worried. "We must take her a big present," they said, "so she does not get angry with us."

So a collection was made and a beautiful chest was bought.

"Now," said the baker, "who will give the present to the witch? I can't go with my weak heart and that path to climb."

"Nor can I," said the teacher, "with my bad leg."

Only one voice spoke.

"I'll go," said Lucy. "I'd like to see what she looks like."

"But," said the blacksmith, "won't you be frightened?"

"Oh no," replied Lucy. "My teddy bear will keep me safe."

So Lucy set off to the castle. It was a long climb, but at last she stood before the great doors and knocked.

As she stood there, all by herself, Lucy began to feel just a little bit frightened. But she clutched her old bear and started to sing to keep her spirits up. With a horrible creaking noise, the doors of the castle slowly opened—all by themselves.

Lucy walked straight in.

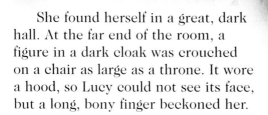

She found herself in a great, dark hall. At the far end of the room, a figure in a dark cloak was crouched on a chair as large as a throne. It wore a hood, so Lucy could not see its face, but a long, bony finger beckoned her.

When the little girl was standing in front of the figure at last, she tried to speak up bravely.

"Please, your highness, or your witchness, we wanted to welcome you to the castle and give you this present."

A horrible cackle came from the dark-robed figure. "A chest? I've got hundreds of them," it croaked. "But I can see that you do have something I want. Give me that teddy bear, and I will let you go home safely."

"No!" cried Lucy, hugging her teddy bear. "You can't have him."

"Really? Then I shall have to lock you up until you agree."

Lucy was dragged into a room with an enormous four-poster bed, and the door was locked behind her.

At dusk, the dark figure brought her some food and a single candle.

"Go to bed," it said.

Lucy climbed into bed. She felt
very frightened, but somehow, she
managed to go to sleep.

At midnight, she was woken by a clock striking by her bed.

Dong! Dong!

She woke to find a large, white bear standing by her bed. He seemed to be shimmering with a strange light.

"W...w...what do you want?" she asked.

The strange bear said nothing, but it held out its paws toward Lucy's little bear, beside her in the bed.

"No!" cried Lucy. "He's mine!"

Then she saw an odd thing. The shining bear was crying!

He looked so very sad that Lucy could not bear it. "All right," she said quietly. "Here's my own special bear to cheer you up."

With a sigh, holding the little bear gently in his arms, the white bear melted through the door! Lucy shut her eyes and rubbed them. When she opened them, she was back in her own room at home, tucked up in her own little bed. Only her teddy bear was missing.

Next morning, the whole village
gathered in amazement at the foot of
the hill. Overnight, the gloomy castle
had changed in an extraordinary way.
The windows sparkled. There were flags
flying from the turrets and doves
fluttering around the battlements.

"It must have
been bewitched
after all," gasped
the villagers. "Our
gift has broken
the spell."

Lucy thought about the chest
hidden under her bed.

"Someone was unhappy," she
thought. "And now they are not. That
is what bears are for."

I believe she was right, my friends.
The mystery never was solved. It was
said that the Countess who lived in
the castle had suffered an unhappy
childhood. Perhaps Lucy gave her
back what she had lost.

The Funny Story of
THE BEAR WHO WAS BARE

My dears, after that scary tale, I have one that is not in the least bit frightening. Uncle Bill Bear here has a much sillier tale to tell you. It is about a bare bear—a bear wearing nothing at all, not even his fur!

Once there was a bear called
Edwin Dalrymple Devereux Yeldon III.
He said that his friends called him
Eddy, but as a matter of fact, this
bear did not have many friends. And
that was because he thought he was
better than other bears, with his long
name and fancy fur.

When the bears played leap-bear or hide-and-seek in the nursery, Eddy always refused to play. "Those are very rough games," he complained. "I might get my paws dirty. Games are too silly for superior bears like myself."

Well, after a while, all the other bears were sick of Edwin and his airs and graces. Some young bears tried to think of ways of teaching Eddy a lesson. But they did not need to. Edwin Dalrymple Devereux Yeldon III brought about his own downfall.

One day, Eddy was boasting about all the famous bears he knew. Some of the other bears wondered out loud if his tales were really true, which made Eddy furious. "You'll see," he said. "I'll write a letter to my friend Prince Bearovski. He's sure to write back at once, and then you'll see."

But as Eddy carried a huge bottle of ink across the room, his furry feet tripped on the edge of the rug. Down fell teddy Eddy. Up flew the bottle of ink. *Splat!* The bottle hit the floor, and ink flew everywhere! There was ink on Eddy's nose and ink on his ears and paws.

Teddy Eddy sulked for the rest of the day. But worse was to follow. Next morning, the little girl who lived there saw what had happened to her most beautiful bear. She decided that Eddy needed a bath.

The other bears peeked around the bathroom door to watch the proceedings. There were bubbles everywhere! Only the tip of teddy Eddy's nose could be seen. The watching bears giggled.

Back in the nursery, the bears waited for Eddy to reappear. But Eddy did not return. Next day, there was no sign of him.

At last the bears went along to the bathroom to see what had happened.

Teddy Eddy was not in the bathtub. The bears were just about to leave, when they noticed that the cupboard was open.

Inside sat Edwin Dalrymple
Devereux Yeldon III, wrapped from
ears to paws in a large towel.

"Come on, Eddy," called the
other bears, "you must be dry by
now, surely?"

"No," said Eddy. "I … er … can't."

"Oh come on," laughed the bears.
And they tugged at the towel. Eddy
tried to hold onto it, but it was no use.
As the towel slipped away, every bear
could see … Edwin Dalrymple
Devereux Yeldon III was bare!

When the little girl washed away
the ink, Eddy's fur was washed away
too. Poor Eddy. He couldn't hide any
more. The old, proud Edwin
Dalrymple Devereux Yeldon III was
gone. A very different bear remained.

For a few days, the other bears
smiled to themselves about what had
happened. But after a while, they
began to feel rather sorry for Eddy.

"I think we should help him," said
one old bear. "He must be cold
without his fur."

"Why don't we make him some
clothes?" said another bear.

Over the next few days, the bears
had great fun. They used up all the
old scraps of material that they could
find and made some very grand clothes.

When he saw them, Eddy was
overwhelmed by the bears' kindness.

"Thank you, my friends," he said,
as he put on the clothes. "I will try to
be a nice bear now. In following all
that is good and kind and bearlike, I
will be absolutely fearless. Or perhaps
I should say, absolutely furless!"

The Short Story of
THE LITTLEST BEAR

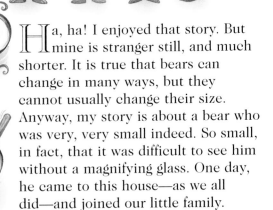

Ha, ha! I enjoyed that story. But mine is stranger still, and much shorter. It is true that bears can change in many ways, but they cannot usually change their size. Anyway, my story is about a bear who was very, very small indeed. So small, in fact, that it was difficult to see him without a magnifying glass. One day, he came to this house—as we all did—and joined our little family.

What? No, there isn't any more to the story. I told you it was short. The bear was so small that he disappeared on the day he came here and has never been seen since. I imagine he is here with us now. Why don't you all take a look around?

The Unusual Story of

THE REAL TEDDY BEAR·

Ben Bear here. My story is about something that happened to me a few years ago, when I met a real teddy bear. Yes, yes, I know that we are all real teddy bears. What I mean is that this was a real live bear—the kind with sharp claws and huge teeth.

Here is what happened. My owner at the time was a little boy who was very fond of food. Wherever we went, he always made sure that he had a bag of goodies with him. Joseph (that was his name) felt happier if he had some provisions with him.

When he went camping with his friends, Joseph took extra supplies.

One year, we went deep into the woods. The boys put up their tents and went off to explore. Joseph left me in his tent. He looked at me very seriously and said, "Now Ben, your job is to stay here and guard the food!" And I was a young bear who took his job seriously in those days.

The boys were gone for a long time. I believe I dozed off for a while, because the next thing I knew, I was wide awake and listening to a very different sound. It was a snorting, sniffling, crunching, munching sort of a noise. I wasn't frightened, of course, but I did wish I knew just what was stomping and chomping outside Joseph's tent.

The sounds got louder and louder. Then I heard the sound of the tent flap being unzipped. *Zoooooooooooop!*

A brown furry face peered in. It was a bear! A real bear!

For a long, long moment, I looked
at the bear. And the bear looked at
me. Then he opened his mouth and
said, "Hello! Anything to eat in here?"

Well, you could have knocked
me down with a feather. He was
speaking bear language, of
course, but I found it was
not very different from
teddy bear language.

Just in time, I
remembered my duty.

"No," I said firmly.
"No food in here
at all."

But the bear was sniffing the air.
"Really?" he said. "I'm pretty sure
I can smell sausages and beans and
chocolate cake."

I thought quickly. "There *were*
sausages and beans and chocolate
cake, but the boys have eaten them."

"Any leftovers?" asked the bear. "Any crumbs at all?"

"None at all," I replied.

The bear nodded his head. "Ho hum," he said. "It's my birthday, you know. I just thought I might find a birthday treat around here. Well, nice meeting you." And as he ambled away into the forest, I'm sure I could hear his furry tummy rumbling.

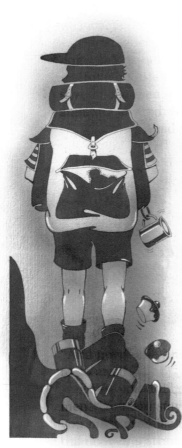

Next morning, as planned, we packed up our things and set off for home.

"Now, have we got everything?" asked Joseph. "Let's go!"

By this stage, of course, I was well hidden in Joseph's backpack, so that the other boys would not see me. Otherwise I might have mentioned to him that the special emergency supplies bag had fallen behind the stump of a tree, helped along just a bit by a nudge from my elbow.

Joseph was a little upset when he
found that his goodies were gone. But
it was far too late to go back into the
dark forest to find them.

As I sat on Joseph's pillow that
night, I looked up at the big
yellow moon peeking in at the
window and imagined the
friendly bear, sitting down
in the moonlight to
enjoy a special snack.

"Happy birthday,
bear," I whispered.
"Happy birthday!"

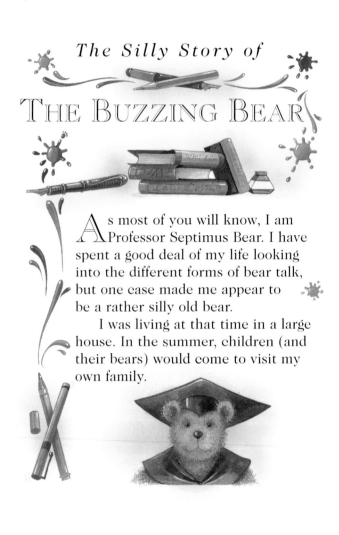

The Silly Story of

THE BUZZING BEAR

As most of you will know, I am Professor Septimus Bear. I have spent a good deal of my life looking into the different forms of bear talk, but one case made me appear to be a rather silly old bear.

I was living at that time in a large house. In the summer, children (and their bears) would come to visit my own family.

That was how I met the buzzing bear. He came to the house on a fine, sunny day. He was a large, fluffy bear, with golden yellow fur. Of course, I tried to make him welcome.

"Good morning," I said. "My name is Septimus. Will you tell me yours?"

"Buzz!" said the bear.

"Er … Buzz? Well, it's nice to meet you, Mr. Buzz. How was your journey?"

"Buzz!" said the bear.

"I'm sorry? Did you say that you have come from far away?"

"Buzz! Buzz! Buzz!" said the strange bear.

I was puzzled. I went straight to my books to find out if there was a country where bears only buzzed.

But all my research was in vain. There are hooting bears in Borneo and some singing bears in Thailand. But I could find nothing at all about buzzing bears.

At first I was disappointed. Then I realized the great opportunity that had been presented to me. I could be the very first bear to study this extraordinary language.

At once, I picked up a new
notebook and pencil and set off to
find the bear.

The buzzing bear was sitting
rather sadly in a chair. I sat down
beside him and began to take notes.

"Are you a bear?" I asked.

"Buzz!" he said.

Ah, I thought, one buzz means yes.

"Are you an elephant?" I asked.

"Buzz! BUZZ!" said the bear.

Two buzzes must mean no.

"Are you a giraffe?" I enquired.

"Buzz!"

My friends, I was very confused.
Then I realized that the bear might
not be able to understand me at all!

It was a beautiful day, so I took the bear by the arm and led him gently out into the garden. By the house was an enormous cedar tree. I led the bear up to it and patted its trunk firmly.

"Tree," I said. "Tree."

"Buzz!" said the bear.

I walked over to a shady seat.

"Chair," I repeated, pointing. "Chair. Chair."

You can probably guess what the bear said.

After half an hour, I had made no progress at all, and I was afraid that my reputation as a scholar was at stake.

At last, I invited the bear to sit down by a flower border.

We had only been sitting for a moment when, "Buzz! BUZZ!" Out of the strange bear's ears flew two big buzzing bees!

"What a relief!" said the bear. "I haven't been able to hear a thing with those bees buzzing in there!"

The Strange Story of

THE ADVENTUROUS BEAR

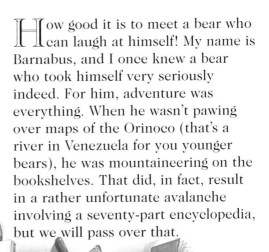

How good it is to meet a bear who can laugh at himself! My name is Barnabus, and I once knew a bear who took himself very seriously indeed. For him, adventure was everything. When he wasn't pawing over maps of the Orinoco (that's a river in Venezuela for you younger bears), he was mountaineering on the bookshelves. That did, in fact, result in a rather unfortunate avalanche involving a seventy-part encyclopedia, but we will pass over that.

Now, strangely enough, one of the
volumes of the encyclopedia fell open
at a page about a man who went
around the world in eighty days. No
sooner had he read this, than our
friend—let's call him B.—decided he
would be the very first bear to travel
right around the world.

"You will need to beware of
sharks," said an old seafaring bear.

"You will have to look out for
icebergs," said another. "The white
bears who live on them are very fierce."

"Don't forget to send us some
postcards," said a little bear.

B. spent months preparing for his trip. By the time he was ready, he had so much equipment, he could hardly walk.

"Good luck!" everyone called, as he staggered off.

Well, eighty days passed. And then another eighty. There was no news from the adventurer.

Then, one morning, a postcard arrived. It showed a picture of the Eiffel Tower. On the back, there were just three words: *Reached France. B.*

The following month, a postcard showed the Leaning Tower of Pisa. The message said: *Crossing Italy. B.*

A few weeks later, a card showed the Great Wall of China, with the message: *Learning Chinese. B.*

Next month, the excited bears waited for a postcard to drop onto the doormat. At last it came, showing a Spanish flamenco dancer. The message read: *In Spain. B.*

The older bears looked puzzled and shook their furry heads. Sure enough, when they looked closely at the postcards, everyone could see that all of them had been sent from a town just a few miles away.

"I think some of us need to go on an expedition too," said the older bears.

This time, the bear expedition returned before nightfall, bringing with them a very crestfallen young bear.

"I did try," he said, "but the world is *so* big!"

The oldest bear put a fatherly arm around my shoulders. "We are just happy to have you home," he said. "Come in and tell us all about your adventures."

Oh, I see that I have given the secret away!

Yes, my friends, I was that foolish young bear. And I can tell you I am happier to be here with you than in Turkey or Tasmania or Thailand!

The Christmas Story of
BEARS EVERYWHERE

Mungo here! My story reminds us of a time of year that is very special for bears. Yes, I mean Christmas. Many bears move to new homes then, as they are given as presents. But we bears have a special job to do at Christmas.

Now, you know that humans make the kind of mistakes that sensible bears would never make. At Christmas time they are worse than ever. Sooner or later, some silly human is likely to send the wrong present to the wrong person.

We bears, who understand how important it is to feel loved and wanted, know that someone who receives the wrong present will feel upset. So that is why our special job at Christmas is to look out for misplaced presents and send them back to where they belong.

One Christmas, a forgetful granny in England made a particularly bad mistake. She sent woolly gloves to her niece in Australia, where it is hot at Christmas time, and a sunhat to her niece in Canada, where the snow lay thick on the ground. And to make matters worse, she sent them at the very last minute.

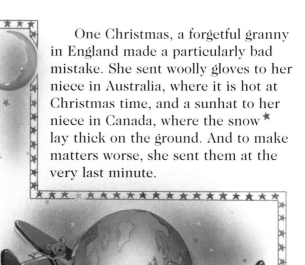

What could we bears do with so little time to spare? Even last-minute flights from both countries would not arrive in time. A council meeting of the Growling was called at once, and the Oldest Bear of All was consulted.

"Dear bears," he said, in his quavering voice, "I can see only one solution, and it is one that we can use only in the most serious cases. These presents will have to be … *ahem* … lost … until Christmas is over. Please alert the bears concerned at once."

Just as soon as messages could reach the bears at opposite sides of the world, action was taken.

The parcel with the gloves was dropped carefully behind a cushion. The package containing the sunhat was tucked into a cupboard.

Now normally in this kind of situation, action is taken immediately after Christmas. The presents are exchanged and then allowed to be discovered. But for some reason, both sets of bears in this case forgot all about the "missing" presents.

In fact, it was not until six months later that teddy bears in Australia discovered the offending package. In horror, they at once contacted their Canadian cousins, and that parcel was retrieved as well. Now both sets of bears were at a loss to know what to do.

The bears reported to the next meeting of the Growling. There were gasps of horror around the room. Then the Oldest Bear of All told those bears what he thought of them.

"Sir," said one of the guilty bears, "we will make the exchange at once."

But at this the Oldest Bear smiled. "I think you will find," he said, "that no exchange will now be necessary. Simply allow the presents to be found. But make sure that this NEVER happens again."

The bears did as they were told. The niece in Australia was delighted with her gloves. The niece in Canada just loved her sunhat. Which of you clever bears can tell me why the presents did not need to be changed?

The Secret Story of

THE BEARS WHO WERE BRAVE

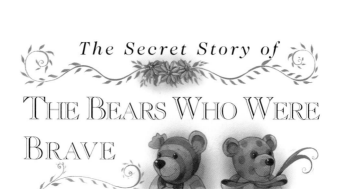

After that *seasonal* story, Mungo, it is my turn. My name is Bella Bear, and my story tells of two bears who both did a very brave thing.

The first bear was called Walter. He was a very fine bear in every way, but he was very afraid of dogs. When he was young, a poodle chewed one of his ears and he never got over it.

The second bear was Hannah. She simply could not stand heights.

Both Hannah and Walter lived with a little boy called Joshua. But when Joshua's baby sister was born, Joshua said he was too old for teddy bears, and he gave them to the baby.

In fact, Joshua was a little bit upset by the amount of attention that the baby received, so his parents gave him a baby of his own—a little puppy called Jack. Jack went everywhere with Joshua, and he really was rather like a baby. He whimpered when he was hungry, and he made little puddles!

One day, Walter and Hannah were left in the garden at lunchtime.

Suddenly, the bears heard a frightened little bark. Somehow, the naughty puppy had managed to climb onto the roof of the summerhouse. He was stuck.

"We must rescue that puppy," said Hannah.

"Hmph," said Walter.

"Joshua loves him," Hannah reminded him.

"All right," said Walter, "but you can do it, because I'm not going anywhere near him."

"But I can't go up there!" cried Hannah. "It's much too high!"

The two little bears sat miserably together. Then both spoke at once.

"I'll go if you will," they said.

So Hannah and Walter helped each other up onto the summerhouse roof and showed the silly puppy how to get down.

None of the humans in the house know how brave the little bears were. But the puppy knew, and I think he told Joshua, because a few days later, the little boy decided that his sister was too *small* for bears, and he tucked Hannah and Walter into *his* bed again.

The Sleepy Story of

THE BEAR WHO
COULDN'T STAY AWAKE

My friends, the fire is burning low and the smallest bears have fallen asleep on our laps. Let's have one more story and then go to bed.

My story is of a very sleepy bear called Selina. She was always to be found dozing in a corner. But when there was a treat in store, Selina was always awake! When there was tidying to be done, or honeypots to wash, Selina would be snoring quietly somewhere.

"If you ask me," grumbled the Oldest Bear of All, "that lazy little bear is just pretending. She needs to be taught a lesson."

"Bears do need their sleep," explained her friend Marilyn. "And Selina has slept right through suppertime. She wouldn't do that if she was really awake. She's always very hungry."

The older bears shook their heads. "If she is pretending," they said, "she will wake up after we are asleep and have a little snack then. We must stay awake tonight and watch."

As it grew dark, five bears took up their positions and watched the sleeping Selina.

Very soon, the first little bear's bright eyes began to close. In just two minutes, he was fast asleep.

The second little bear struggled hard to stay awake, but soon he too was dreaming a teddy-bear dream.

The third bear was older than the first two. He was quite determined to stay awake. He decided to march up and down—quietly, of course. *Pad, pad, pad*, he marched across the floor. *Pad, pad, pad*, back he came. *Pad, pad, pad ... pad, pad, pad.* He looked as if he was awake. He sounded as if he was awake. But that bear was sleep-walking!

The fourth and fifth watching bears decided to keep each other awake. They talked in whispers late into the night. But soon the whispers became gentle snores.

In the morning, the other bears crowded round.

"Well … *ahem*," said the first bear, "I certainly didn't see her wake up."

"Er … neither did I," agreed the second bear.

"I was on duty all night," said the third bear, "and I didn't hear a sound."

"I saw nothing unusual," said the fourth bear, truthfully.

"Nor did I," replied his friend.

So the mystery of the sleeping bear never was solved. But Selina gave an extra loud snore and the tiniest, sleepy, secret smile.

Now it is time for little bears everywhere to go to sleep. Goodnight, little bears! Goodnight!

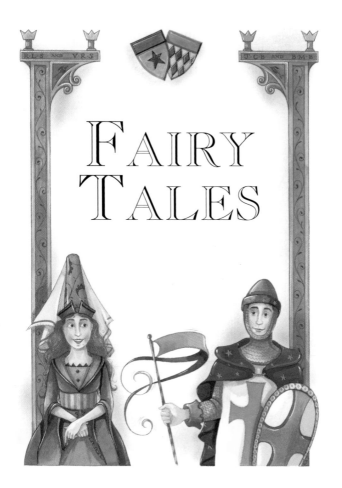

FAIRY
TALES

Hansel and Gretel

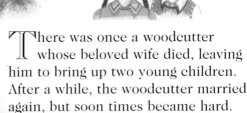

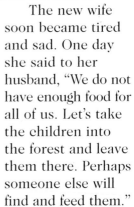

There was once a woodcutter whose beloved wife died, leaving him to bring up two young children. After a while, the woodcutter married again, but soon times became hard.

The new wife soon became tired and sad. One day she said to her husband, "We do not have enough food for all of us. Let's take the children into the forest and leave them there. Perhaps someone else will find and feed them."

Meanwhile, the woodcutter's children had been listening..

"Don't worry, Gretel," said the little boy, whose name was Hansel.

The next day, the family went deep into the forest. As they walked, Hansel dropped crumbs from a crust, hoping to follow them back home again. But the birds soon ate the crumbs, and when the children were left all alone in the forest, they were completely lost.

Hungry and afraid, Hansel and Gretel wandered through the trees. Suddenly, they saw a cottage made of candy and gingerbread!

But no sooner had the children munched into the house, than a sharp voice shouted, "Eat your fill, dear children!"

It was a witch! She bundled the children into her house.

The witch made Gretel work for her, while she kept Hansel in a cage. Every day, she asked him to poke his finger out of the cage to see if he was fat enough to eat!

At last the day came when the witch could wait no longer. "Stoke up the fire," she said to Gretel, "and put your head in the oven to see if it is hot enough."

But Gretel said, "You'd better check yourself."

When the witch poked her head into the oven, Gretel gave her a huge push and slammed the door shut.

Quick as a flash, Gretel set her
brother free. Gathering up the witch's
treasure, the children ran from the
house. A little bird showed them the
way home. Their stepmother had gone
back to her own people, but their
father was overjoyed to see them.

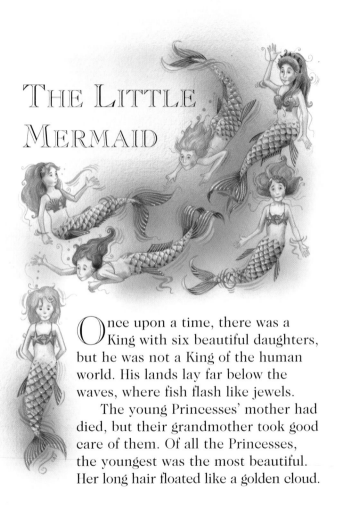

THE LITTLE MERMAID

Once upon a time, there was a King with six beautiful daughters, but he was not a King of the human world. His lands lay far below the waves, where fish flash like jewels.

The young Princesses' mother had died, but their grandmother took good care of them. Of all the Princesses, the youngest was the most beautiful. Her long hair floated like a golden cloud.

The girls loved to hear their grandmother tell them stories of the land above the waves. There, she told them, human beings walked on strange things called legs.

The youngest mermaid longed to see it.

"When you are fifteen," her grandmother said, "you shall go."

When the eldest Princess was old enough, she swam to the surface, returning the next day to tell of the wonderful things she had seen.

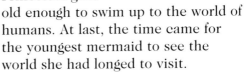

Year after year, one after another, the mermaid Princesses grew old enough to swim up to the world of humans. At last, the time came for the youngest mermaid to see the world she had longed to visit.

As she rose to the surface for the first time, the sun was just setting. Nearby, a fine ship was sailing. As the little mermaid watched, a handsome Prince came onto the deck. He did not know that he was being watched, or that the little mermaid could not take her eyes from his face.

Darkness fell, and the ship began to toss as the wind rose. A dreadful storm wrenched away the sails and the rigging, and huge waves crashed onto the deck. As the ship sank, the little mermaid saw the Prince, struggling in the water. She held up his head and guided him gently to shore. When morning came, the wind dropped and the sun rose. The little mermaid stayed near the shore to watch over the sleeping Prince.

Before long, some girls came along. The Prince woke as they bent over him on the sand. Only the little mermaid felt sad.

After that, the little mermaid often rose to the surface, eager for a sight of the Prince. At last, she could not bear it any more. She decided to go to see the powerful Water Witch.

The Water Witch laughed when she saw the little mermaid. "I know why you have come," she said. "You want to go and live in the human world, so that you can be near the Prince. But do you know the price you will have to pay?"

"No," whispered the Princess, "but I will pay it gladly to be human."

"I shall need your voice, with which you sing so sweetly," said the witch.

"Then I can turn you into a lovely human girl. But remember, if the Prince does not love you with all his heart and take you for his wife, you will turn into sea foam and be lost forever."

"Hurry," said the mermaid. "I have already decided."

So the Water Witch gave the little mermaid a potion to drink.

As soon as the little mermaid stood for the first time before the Prince she loved, he wanted to meet her and, although she could not speak to him, he soon found that he could not bear to be apart from her.

The little mermaid loved the young man more each day, but he never thought of marrying her.

Months passed, and the Prince's mother and father urged him to find a bride. At last he agreed to meet a Princess in a nearby country. Of course, the little mermaid went with him, but she felt as if her heart were breaking.

When the Prince stepped on shore
and met the new Princess for the first
time, he was so dazzled by her beauty
that he decided to marry her at once.

The wedding was a magnificent
affair, with flowers and silks and
jewels. Everyone cheered
with joy to see the
happy pair. Only
the little mermaid
was silent. Her
tears fell
unseen.

That night, the little mermaid stood on deck and gazed at the dark water. At dawn, she would be turned into foam.

But as she stood there, her sisters rose to the surface of the water. Their flowing hair was cut short.

"We gave it to the Water Witch," they said, "in return for this knife. If you kill the Prince tonight, you will be free of the spell."

The little mermaid took the knife, but, as dawn broke, she knew that she could never harm the Prince.

Weeping, the little
mermaid plunged into
the sea, but instead of
turning into foam,
she found herself
floating in the air.
Around her were
lovely creatures
made of golden light.

"We are the
daughters of the
air," they said.
"You can be
happy at last
with us."

As the little mermaid rose into the
sunshine, she looked down at the
Prince's ship and she smiled.

SLEEPING BEAUTY

Once there lived a King and Queen who were overjoyed when a baby girl was born to them.

It seemed as though everyone in the kingdom was invited to a grand feast for her. The most important guests were the twelve fairies who make special wishes for children.

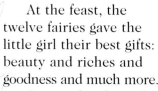

At the feast, the twelve fairies gave the little girl their best gifts: beauty and riches and goodness and much more.

Just as the eleventh fairy had finished her wish, there was a crash as the door swung open. It was the thirteenth fairy, whom everyone had forgotten.

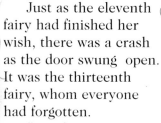

"Here's my present!" she screeched. "On her fifteenth birthday, the Princess will prick her finger on a spindle and die! That will teach you to forget me!"

As the guests looked at each other in horror, the twelfth fairy spoke.

"I can make the curse a little better," she said. "The Princess will prick her finger, but she will not die. Instead, she will fall asleep for a hundred years."

The years passed, and the Princess grew up to be clever, kind, and beautiful. On her fifteenth birthday, she woke up early.

Outside, she noticed a little door she had never seen before. She opened it and climbed eagerly up the stairs inside.

At the top of the stairs was a very old woman. Now the Princess had never seen anyone spinning before, for the King had banished all spindles from the kingdom.

"Would you like to try?" the old woman asked, holding out the spindle to the curious girl.

As she took the spindle, the Princess pricked her finger and at once fell asleep. At the same moment, everyone in the castle fell asleep as well—even the hunting dogs!

Many, many years later—exactly one hundred, in fact—a Prince happened to be passing the castle. It was so overgrown with brambles that you could only see the topmost turrets. But as he rode along beside the high, thorny hedge, it burst into bloom and opened to let the Prince through.

The Prince soon found himself in the small room where the Princess was sleeping. He could not resist bending to kiss her.

At that moment, the hundred years came to an end. The Princess opened her eyes, and saw a handsome young man, smiling down at her.

It was not long before the Prince and Princess were married. This time, the King was very careful indeed with his invitations!

THUMBELINA

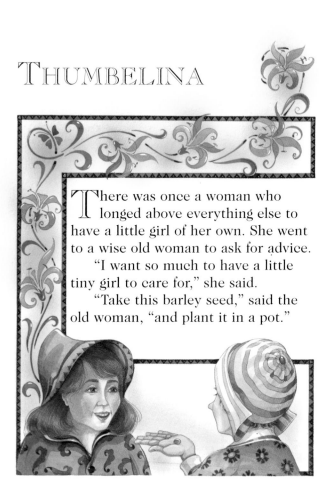

There was once a woman who longed above everything else to have a little girl of her own. She went to a wise old woman to ask for advice.

"I want so much to have a little tiny girl to care for," she said.

"Take this barley seed," said the old woman, "and plant it in a pot."

So the woman
went home and
planted the seed.
It quickly grew into
a strong plant, with
one large bud. When
the flower opened,
the astonished
woman saw a little tiny girl, perfect in
every way, sitting in the middle.

Because she was no bigger than the
woman's thumb, she was called
Thumbelina.

There never was a little girl who
was loved so much or cared for so well.
She had a walnut shell for a cradle and
rose leaves for a blanket.

As her mother worked around the house during the day, Thumbelina played on the table. She had a shallow dish of water, with a lily leaf in the middle, and she loved to sing as she rowed herself back and forth in the sunlight from the open window.

But one night a mother toad hopped through the window and saw the tiny girl in her pretty bed.

"She would make a beautiful wife for my son," thought the toad.

The toad carried the sleeping girl away and put her on a lily leaf in the middle of the river. The little girl was not frightened, but she did not want to marry the toad's son.

Thumbelina sat on her leaf and sobbed. A little fish popped up his head.

"You cannot marry that ugly old toad," he said.

And he bit through the stem of the lily leaf so that it went floating down the river. Thumbelina felt happier now. She passed many beautiful places, and a butterfly flew down to visit her.

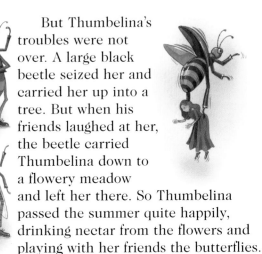

But Thumbelina's troubles were not over. A large black beetle seized her and carried her up into a tree. But when his friends laughed at her, the beetle carried Thumbelina down to a flowery meadow and left her there. So Thumbelina passed the summer quite happily, drinking nectar from the flowers and playing with her friends the butterflies.

But gradually, the days began to grow shorter. Winter was coming, and the nights were cold. Thumbelina knew that she could not survive the winter without a home to live in.

Just as the shivering girl began to lose hope, she met a busy little mouse. "You can stay with me, in my little house," said the mouse kindly.

Thumbelina was happy again, until the mouse's friend came to visit. He was a mole who lived underground, and he soon fell in love with Thumbelina.

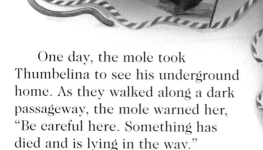

One day, the mole took Thumbelina to see his underground home. As they walked along a dark passageway, the mole warned her, "Be careful here. Something has died and is lying in the way."

It was a bird, but it was still alive! Thumbelina took care of the bird, and by spring, it was ready to fly away to join its friends. The little girl watched it fly away. She knew that when winter came again, she would have to marry the mole and live underground for the rest of her life.

Summer passed again, and Thumbelina stood and looked at the blue sky for the last time. Just then, a voice from above called to her. "Come with me!" It was the bird she had saved!

In no time at all, Thumbelina was sitting on the bird's back, soaring over fields and cities. At last the bird came to rest in a warm, sunny country, where orange trees grew and the air was full of the scent of flowers.

The swallow set Thumbelina down. You can imagine how surprised she was to see a little man, no bigger than herself.

"Welcome to my country," he said. "I am the Prince of all the flower people. We will call you Maia."

The little girl was happy at last.

THE FROG PRINCE

Once there was a King who had seven beautiful daughters.

The youngest was the loveliest. On sunny days, she loved to play with her golden ball by a cool pool in the forest near the castle.

One day, when the Princess threw
her golden ball high into the air,
something dreadful happened. It fell …
SPLASH! … into the water.

"It is lost forever!" the girl cried.

"I could dive down and find
your ball," said a little green frog
by the pool, "if you would promise
that I could be your friend, share your
meals, and snuggle into your bed at night."

"Anything!" gasped the Princess.

But as soon as the frog had given her back the ball, the Princess ran back to the castle.

That evening, the King and his family sat down to supper. Just as they were about to start, there came a croaking at the door. The youngest Princess tried to ignore it.

But the King asked, "Who's there?"

Then the Princess explained about her promise.

"A promise is a promise, my dear," said the King.

So, although the Princess hated to look at him, the frog was allowed onto the table to share her supper.

After supper, the Princess tried to slip off to bed by herself.

"What about me?" croaked a little voice from the table.

"Remember what I said about promises," said the King.

The Princess unwillingly carried the frog to her bedroom and put him down in a corner.

"I'd much rather sit on your pillow," croaked the little creature.

Close to tears, the Princess dropped the frog onto her pillow.

At once, the little green frog turned into a handsome, smiling Prince.

"Don't be afraid," he said. "A wicked witch put a spell on me that only a kind Princess could break. I hope that we can still be friends, now that I am no longer a frog."

A few years later, the Prince and Princess were married, and you can be sure that they invited some very special little green guests!

THE EMPEROR'S NEW CLOTHES

The Emperor in this story was not interested in waging war or building castles, as most Emperors are. He simply loved clothes. It was well known that he spent most of the day trying on one costume after another to find which was most flattering to the (rather generous) royal figure.

One day there came to the court a pair of rascals intent on making a little money and living an easy life. They let it be known that they were weavers. "The cloth that we weave," they said, "is so fine, and its pattern is so intricate, that only intelligent people can see it."

Before long, the Emperor heard of this. "How very useful," he said to himself. "If I wore a suit of that cloth, I would be able to tell at once which of my ministers were too stupid and ill bred for their jobs." So he summoned the weavers before him.

"I would like a suit made of your famous cloth," he told them.

"No problem at all," replied the weavers. "If we could just take a few measurements. My, Your Highness has the figure of a man of twenty!"

Next the weavers ordered bales of costly silk and gold thread, to weave, they said, into their famous cloth. They had two looms set up in a comfortable room. All day they sat in front of the looms, pretending to weave.

The Emperor was anxious to see how his suit was coming along, but although he knew that he was the cleverest man in the land, he was just a little worried that he might not be able to see the cloth.

The Emperor thought long and hard until he had an idea.

"Summon my Chief Minister!" he cried. "He can report to me on the cloth the weavers are making for me."

Well, the Chief Minister couldn't see the cloth either. But he was worried that the Emperor might dismiss him, so he pretended it was wonderful.

Every day, the weavers called for more silk and gold. They packed this away in their luggage, ready for a quick getaway!

Soon the Emperor sent his Chancellor to inspect the work. Once again, the poor man could see nothing at all, but he did not want to lose his job. "It is beyond compare," he declared. "Your Highness will be really delighted."

The Emperor hurried to the weavers' room and flung open the doors.

He stopped dead. It was his worst nightmare! Only he, of all his court, was too stupid to see the wonderful cloth. His throat felt dry as he said, "This cloth is too beautiful for words!"

At the end of the week there was to be a Grand Procession. Naturally, it was expected that the Emperor would wear clothes of the famous new cloth. The weavers were busy night and day, cutting thin air with huge pairs of scissors, sewing with invisible thread, and pretending to sew on buttons.

On the morning of the Grand Procession, the Emperor stood in his underwear while the weavers helped him on with his clothes. By the time he had walked up and down a few times, he had persuaded himself that he could almost see the costume, and that it was very fine indeed.

So it was that the Emperor walked proudly out wearing only his second-best pair of royal underwear.

At first, there was a stunned silence from the crowd lining the streets. But everyone had heard that only clever people could see the clothes, so first one and then another spectator cried out, "Wonderful! Superb!" as the Emperor passed.

Sometimes, when everyone is making a lot of noise, there is suddenly a brief silence. In just such a moment, the voice of a little boy could be heard. "But Mother," he cried, "the Emperor isn't wearing any clothes!"

In that dreadful moment, the crowd realized that it was true, and they began to laugh. The Emperor ran in a most unroyal way back to the palace.

It is said that the Emperor never was quite so vain about clothes after that. And the two rascals? They had become as invisible as the Emperor's costume and were never seen again.

THE FISHERMAN AND HIS WIFE

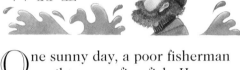

One sunny day, a poor fisherman caught a very fine fish. He was just about to unhook it from his line, when the fish spoke!

"I am not really a fish but an enchanted Prince," he said. "Please put me back in the water."

"Of course," said the fisherman. "I wouldn't dream of eating a talking fish!" He put the fish back in the sea and went home to his wife.

The fisherman and his wife lived in
a rickety old hut near the beach. It was
in a terrible state! Everything was
higgledy piggledy.

When the fisherman
told his wife about the
talking fish, she cried out,
"You silly man! You should
have asked for something
for us in return. Go straight
back and ask for a nice little
cottage to live in."

So the fisherman went back to the seashore. The sun was hidden behind a cloud.

When the fish heard the man's request, he said, "Of course. Your wish is granted."

The fisherman went home. Where his hut used to be was a snug cottage.

At first all was well, but after a couple of weeks, the fisherman's wife said, "I deserve better than this. Go back and ask the fish to give us a castle. I want to be Queen!"

The next day, the fisherman did as she asked. The waves washed angrily against the shore, but the fish listened as before.

"Very well," he said. "Once more, your wish has been granted."

This time, when the fisherman trudged home, he found his wife surrounded by servants in an enormous castle. She seemed to be enjoying herself.

But only a few days later, the fisherman's wife said, "Being Queen is all very well, but I have been thinking...."

The fisherman's heart sank, as he set off for the seashore once again. The sea was very dark and stormy when he reached the water.

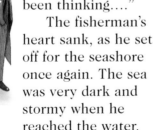

"Oh fish!" called the fisherman.
"My wife wants to be Empress of the
Earth and Sky."

"Go home," said the fish. "Your
wife has all that she deserves."

And when he reached home, what
did the fisherman find? Just a rickety
old hut and his wife inside, complaining.

And the fisherman has not seen the
talking fish from that day to this,
although he looks for him all the time.

THE PRINCESS AND THE PEA

Once upon a time, there was a Prince who had very firm views about Princesses.

"Many of them are simply not Princesses at all," he said airily.

"My dear, whatever do you mean?" asked his mother the Queen. "We have met lots of charming girls."

"No. Princess Petunia spoke unkindly to her maid. Princess Pearl was *silly*. And Princess Petronella talked all the time and never listened to a word anyone else said. They weren't *real* Princesses. Real Princesses are … well, they're … that is, they seem … oh, I don't know!"

"I do wish he could meet someone
and settle down," sighed the King, as
the Prince rushed from the room. "But
how are we ever to be sure that a girl
is a real Princess?"

"My dear," said the Queen,
"just leave that to me."

That year, the Prince visited many countries and met many Princesses, but he found fault with every one of them. At last he returned home, sad and tired.

One night, as the royal family sat in front of a roaring fire, there came a knocking at the door of the castle.

"Some poor fellow is out in the storm," said the King. "We must let him in to warm himself."

The King pulled open the door himself.

Outside stood a rain-drenched figure. The King had to peer more closely to see that it was a young girl in a thin cloak.

"My dear child," cried the King. "Come in at once!"

"My carriage overturned, and I was forced to go in search of shelter," said the girl, as she came inside. "And you'd be surprised how few people are ready to help a real Princess knocking on their door."

"Did you say a *real* Princess?" asked the King, looking at his wife.

"Of course," his visitor replied. "My father is a King."

"Well, well," said the King. "I wonder, have you met my son, the Prince?"

As the Prince came forward to greet the girl who made his heart stand still, the Queen hurried off to have her room prepared.

Half an hour later, the Princess was tucked up in her room.

The King could not wait to consult his wife.

"Well?" he whispered. "What do you think? The boy seems rather taken with her, but is she real?"

"We'll soon know about that," said the Queen. "I have put twenty mattresses on her bed. Below the bottom one I have placed a dried pea. Now we shall see what we shall see."

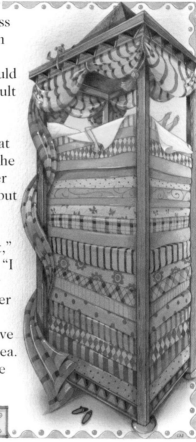

Next morning, the members of the royal family looked up eagerly as their visitor entered the room.

"My dear," said the Queen, "I hope you had a restful night."

"I'm afraid not," replied the girl, "although you made me so welcome and comfortable. I tossed and turned all night long, and this morning I am black and blue. It's as though there was a boulder under my mattresses."

At that the Queen beamed at her son. "Here," she said, "is a real Princess, my boy. Only a girl with truly royal blood would have skin so tender that she could feel a tiny pea through twenty mattresses. You have my blessing."

Luckily, it was soon discovered
that the Princess had fallen as much in
love with the Prince as he had with her.

They were married soon after, amid
great rejoicing. And the royal museum
still contains a rather wrinkled green
exhibit. You can see it for yourself.

THE ELVES AND THE SHOEMAKER

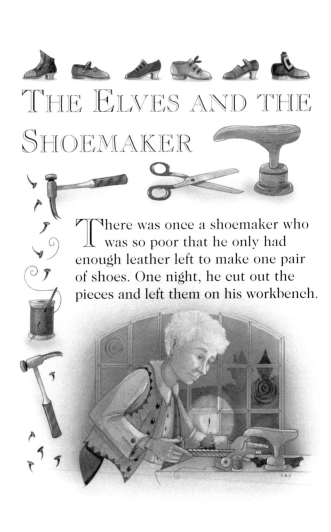

There was once a shoemaker who was so poor that he only had enough leather left to make one pair of shoes. One night, he cut out the pieces and left them on his workbench.

The next morning, the shoemaker came downstairs to begin work. He was amazed to find that the leather had already been made into shoes!

The poor man couldn't understand what had happened, but he proudly put the shoes in his window. Within an hour, a very rich customer had seen the shoes and bought them.

"Now I have enough money to buy leather for two pairs of shoes," the shoemaker told his wife.

The next morning, the shoemaker and his wife could hardly wait to creep down into the workshop. Sure enough, there on the workbench were two pairs of dainty shoes. "I've never seen such fine workmanship," gasped the shoemaker.

Once again, he had no trouble in selling the shoes for a handsome price. From that day onward, the shoemaker's troubles were ended. Soon his shop was busy all the time.

One day, near Christmas, the shoemaker's wife said, "I've been thinking that we should try to find out who has been helping us all this time."

The shoemaker agreed. That night, instead of going to bed, he and his wife hid behind the workbench and waited to see what would happen.

At midnight, the door opened and in danced two little men. They were dressed in rags, but they cheerfully sat down and began to sew. Before dawn, they slipped out into the street.

"So now we know," smiled the shoemaker.

"Surely, the least we can do to thank them is to make them some new clothes," said his wife. "And you could make them some little shoes."

A few nights later, the tiny presents were finished. The shoemaker and his wife hid as before.

Just after midnight, the little men appeared. At the sight of the clothes, they danced with happiness.

*"Now that we
Are such fine men,
We need not come
To work again!"*

they sang, and they skipped out of the shop, never to return.

THE SNOW QUEEN

There was once a mirror belonging to a magician. It made everything look ugly and twisted, no matter how beautiful it really was. One day, the mirror broke, and thousands of tiny pieces went flying across the world. Some flew into people's eyes and made everything look spoiled and dirty. Others were tiny sharp slivers that flew into people's hearts. They turned them to ice, so that they could not feel love and happiness anymore.

Meanwhile, a little girl and boy who lived opposite each other were playing happily high above the busy street. Their houses almost touched, and there were window boxes on the top floor. In the summer, the little girl, who was called Gerda, and the little boy, who was called Kay, played together in their tiny garden.

In the winter, when the windows were shut, they watched the snowflakes swirling through the window like a flock of bees.

"There is a Queen of the Snow just as there is a Queen Bee," said Grandmother. "She is the biggest snow-flake, whirling in the storm."

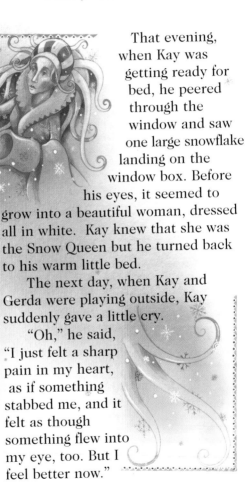

That evening, when Kay was getting ready for bed, he peered through the window and saw one large snowflake landing on the window box. Before his eyes, it seemed to grow into a beautiful woman, dressed all in white. Kay knew that she was the Snow Queen but he turned back to his warm little bed.

The next day, when Kay and Gerda were playing outside, Kay suddenly gave a little cry.

"Oh," he said, "I just felt a sharp pain in my heart, as if something stabbed me, and it felt as though something flew into my eye, too. But I feel better now."

Tiny pieces of the magician's mirror were now lodged in Kay's eye and heart, which was turned to ice. Seeing Gerda's worried little face, Kay spoke coldly.

"What's the matter with you, Gerda? You don't look at all pretty like that. I'm going off to play with the other boys in the square."

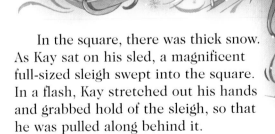

In the square, there was thick snow. As Kay sat on his sled, a magnificent full-sized sleigh swept into the square. In a flash, Kay stretched out his hands and grabbed hold of the sleigh, so that he was pulled along behind it.

As the sleigh flew over the fields, the snow swirled thicker around Kay. He began to be rather frightened.

At last the strange sleigh stopped, and the white figure driving it stood up. Kay could see that it was the Snow Queen, dressed in a cloak of white fur.

Kay was no longer afraid but flew on with her in the moonlight.

Back in the city, little Gerda
learned that Kay had disappeared.
Everyone said that he must be dead,
but Gerda could not believe that. As
soon as spring arrived, she set off to
find Kay in her new red shoes.

Gerda soon reached the countryside.
Before long, she saw a large orchard,
full of cherry trees, and an old
woman wearing a straw hat,
covered with flowers.

Gerda was glad
to see a friendly face.
Soon she had told
the woman about Kay.

"I haven't seen
him, but you can stay
here and wait," said
the woman.

In fact, the old woman really wanted to look after a little girl just like Gerda. She was careful to magic away all the roses in her garden, so that Gerda was not reminded of home.

But the old lady had forgotten about her hat! One day, Gerda noticed that one of the flowers on it was a rose. "Oh, no!" cried the little girl. "I have wasted so much time."

Without even waiting to put on her shoes, Gerda ran out of the garden. Her feet were soon sore, so she sat down to rest near a large raven.

"I may have seen Kay," said the raven, "but he has forgotten you. He thinks only of the Princess."

"Is he living with a Princess?" asked Gerda.

Then the raven told her about a Princess who was very clever. She advertised for a husband, and before long, the castle was packed with young men lining up to see her. Unfortunately, when they came into her presence, all of them were too overcome to say a word, so she sent them away.

"But what about Kay?" asked Gerda.
Then the raven told how a boy who was not afraid of anyone came along and delighted the Princess by talking with her about all the things that interested her.

"Oh, that must be Kay. He is so clever," said Gerda. "I must see him!"

"I will see what I can do," cawed the raven, and he flew away.

At evening, the raven came back. "Come quickly!" he said.

So Gerda hurried to the castle, where the raven's sweetheart was waiting. She crept up the back stairs. past swift shadows of horses and knights.

At last Gerda reached the Princess's room. There, sleeping soundly, was a young man. But it wasn't Kay!

Gerda was so disappointed that she burst into tears, waking the Prince and Princess. They felt sorry for the little girl and did what they could to help her. They gave her some new boots and a golden carriage, with footmen to take her on her way.

But Gerda's adventures were not over. As she passed in her carriage through a dark forest, some robbers jumped out. They could see that the carriage was worth a fortune. Those robbers might well have killed Gerda at once, but a little robber girl took her back to her home.

That night Gerda heard some wood pigeons cooing. "We have seen little Kay riding through the sky in the Snow Queen's sleigh."

The little robber girl's pet reindeer said quietly, "The Snow Queen has her summer palace near the North Pole. I know, for I was born near there."

The next morning, the little robber girl spoke to Gerda. "I heard everything last night," she said. "I will let the reindeer go if he will promise to carry you to Lapland to find Kay."

The reindeer jumped for joy, and Gerda climbed on his back. Night and day they flew through the forest and mountains, until the reindeer pointed out the beautiful northern lights and told Gerda that they had arrived in Lapland. There was a poor cottage nearby.

"You poor child," said the woman who lived there. "I'm afraid you have many miles to go yet."

Once again, Gerda and the
reindeer flew over the snowy
landscape, until they reached Finland.
There they met a Finnish woman,
who was a friend of the woman in
Lapland.

"Can't you give Gerda some
special magic, so that she can defeat
the Snow Queen?" asked the reindeer.

"Gerda doesn't need any special
magic," said the Finnish woman. "Her
good heart is all the magic she needs.
Kay is with the Snow Queen. He is
happy there because he has a heart of
ice and a fragment of the magician's
mirror in his eye. Take Gerda to the
edge of the Snow Queen's garden and put
her down by a bush with red berries."

The reindeer did as the Finnish woman suggested, although he was sorry to leave Gerda all alone in the cold snow with her bare feet.

Almost at once, Gerda was surrounded by whirling snowflakes. Some seemed to threaten her but others led her on.

And so it was that Gerda came at last to the Snow Queen's palace, with its walls of snow and doors and windows of bitter winds. Only Gerda's goodness kept her warm as she walked into a huge ice chamber.

There in the middle was little Kay, moving blocks of ice around as if he was trying to solve the hardest puzzle in the world.

Gerda ran forward. As she threw her arms around Kay, her warm tears of joy dripped onto his face and heart, melting the ice and washing away the slivers of mirror. The warmth gradually returned to his cheeks, and he too cried at the sight of his very best friend.

Outside, the reindeer was waiting. The children began their long journey home. At last they saw their own city stretching out before them.

Gerda and Kay were older and wiser, but in their hearts they were children still, and all around them was warmth and light and summer.

THE MUSICIANS OF BREMEN

Once there was a donkey who was old and tired. It became clear that his master would not keep him for much longer.

"The best thing for me to do," thought the donkey, "would be to go to Bremen and become a musician My braying has often been admired."

So early one morning, the donkey set off. On the way, he met a dog, sheltering by a wall.

"I am too old to go hunting with my master," growled the dog. "Now, he hardly feeds me at all."

"Come with me to Bremen!" laughed the donkey. "If I bray and you bark, we shall make fine music!"

And off they went. Before long, they met a cat, crouched on a roof.

"I am old and even the mice laugh at me," mewed the cat pitifully.

"Come with us and be a musician!" called the donkey and the dog. "Your voice is still strong and tuneful, you know."

Now the musicians
made a loud noise as they
went along, but when they
passed by a farmer's barn,
they heard a noise that
was so loud, it drowned
even their strange and
wonderful singing.

"Cock-a-doodle-doo!"
"I am crowing," called the rooster.
"because the farmer is having friends
to dinner tonight. I'm very much
afraid that I'm the main course!"

"Don't worry," the donkey replied.
"I can think of a much better use for
your voice. You just come along with us."

By the evening, the animals were tired. They needed a place to sleep and a fine dinner. At last, they saw the lighted window of a little cottage.

When they reached it, the rooster flew up and looked in the window.

"I can see four robbers, sitting down to a delicious meal!" he called.

"I have a plan," said the donkey.

So the animals climbed on each others' backs. Then they went right up to the window and sang their music at the tops of their voices.

"It's a ghost!" cried one robber.

"It's a goblin!" cried another.

"It's a troll!" called the third.

"I want my mother!" sobbed the last robber.

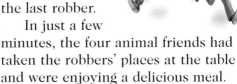

In just a few minutes, the four animal friends had taken the robbers' places at the table and were enjoying a delicious meal.

Later that night, the animals slept soundly in the cottage. But the robbers crept back to see if the coast was clear. The animals were waiting.

As soon as the robbers were inside the cottage, the donkey cried, "Now!" and the animals attacked!

Well, those robbers ran away even faster than they had the first time, leaving the four friends in peace. The cottage was so charming that they never did reach Bremen, but they made time for their singing practice every day. And if you had ever heard them, you would know that the good people of Bremen had a very lucky escape indeed!

THE EMPEROR AND THE NIGHTINGALE

Long ago, the great empire of
China had a mighty Emperor.
His palace and his gardens were
truly magnificent.

At the end of the gardens was a wonderful forest, and beyond the forest the deep blue sea stretched far away. It was here, at the edge of the water, that a nightingale had made her home. Each evening she opened her heart and sang so beautifully that even the fishermen stopped their work to hear her liquid notes.

Many strangers came to the palace and every visitor who heard the nightingale's song could not help exclaiming, "Everything here is wonderful but nothing compares to the song of this magical bird."

When they returned home, some of the visitors wrote books about the place.

Now the Emperor was very fond of reading about his amazing palace and its grounds. You can imagine his surprise when he first read an account that rated the nightingale's song more highly than all his costly possessions.

"Why have I never heard the song of this bird, although she lives within my grounds?" he asked his courtiers. "Bring her to me tonight, for I must hear her sing."

The courtiers had never heard of the nightingale. They ran all over the palace, but they could find no one who had heard her.

The courtiers were almost at their wits' ends when they found a young maid in the Emperor's kitchens.

"I have heard the nightingale sing many times, when I go down to the shore to visit my mother," she said. "It is a truly wonderful sound."

The courtiers insisted that the kitchen maid lead them to the nightingale's tree. As they walked through the forest they heard a deep, booming sound.

"We have found the nightingale," they cried.

"No," said the maid. "It's a cow!"

The courtiers heard a bubbling, chirping sound.

"There's the nightingale," they declared.

"No, that's a frog!" said the maid.

Just then the nightingale began to
sing. A ribbon of beautiful sound
shimmered in the air. The kitchen
maid pointed to a little brown
bird on a branch.

"That is the nightingale," she said.

The courtiers were amazed, but
they invited her to the palace that
evening, as the Emperor had ordered.
The whole court gathered that evening.

As the nightingale's first notes
trembled in the air, tears rolled
down the Emperor's cheeks. He had
never heard anything so beautiful.
The little bird was a great success.

After that, the nightingale had to live at the palace. She had her own golden cage and twelve servants. Twice a day, she was allowed to fly around a little, but one of the servants kept hold of a silken thread attached to her leg.

One day, a present arrived for the Emperor. It was a mechanical bird, made of gold and silver and precious jewels. When it was wound up with a golden key, the bird sang one of the nightingale's songs. It was a gift from the Emperor of Japan.

The mechanical bird sang very well, and always exactly the same song.

The Emperor was persuaded that this bird was the best.

The real nightingale took advantage of the commotion caused by the mechanical bird to fly through the window and back to its old, free life. Only the poor people, who were sometimes allowed to hear the mechanical bird, shook their heads and said, "No, there is something missing. This is not as beautiful as the real bird."

A year passed. One day when the mechanical bird was wound up with the golden key as usual, it merely said, "Krrrrr." The bird had sung so often that its mechanism was worn out. Luckily, the Court Watchmaker was able to repair the bird, but he warned that in future she must only sing once a year.

Several years passed, and the people of China were shocked to learn that their Emperor was very ill. The courtiers were so sure that he was about to die that they began to pay court to the man who would be the next Emperor.

In the middle of the night, the Emperor was visited by fears and phantoms. "Sing!" he begged the mechanical nightingale at his side, but there was no one to wind up the metal bird, so it remained silent.

Suddenly, through the open window, the Emperor heard a wonderful sound.

It was the real nightingale, singing her heart out. As she sang, the Emperor's fevered mind was soothed, and his illness left him.

"Thank you, little bird," he gasped. "You must remain in my palace and sing to me every day."

"No, My Lord," said the bird. "I cannot live in a palace, but I will come of my own free will and sing outside your window. And I will tell you what the poorest people in your land are thinking and feeling, which will make you the wisest Emperor who has ever lived."

The Emperor ruled for many more years, more wisely and well than ever before.

LITTLE RED RIDING HOOD

Once there was a little girl who lived on the edge of a huge forest. One day, her grandmother gave her a beautiful red cape with a hood. The little girl wore it all the time, so she was called Little Red Riding Hood.

One morning, Little Red Riding Hood's mother heard that the grandmother was not feeling well.

"Run along the forest path with this basket of food, Little Red Riding Hood," she said. "Your grandmother will feel better as soon as she sees you. But remember, you must go straight there and don't stop for anything."

Now Little Red Riding Hood had not gone very far, when out of the trees stepped a very large wolf!

"Why, Little Red Riding Hood," he said, "where are you off to?"

The little girl answered politely, "I am going to see my grandmother, but I'm afraid I cannot stop to talk." And on she went.

But when she was halfway to her grandmother's house, Little Red Riding Hood saw the wolf again. He said, "How nice it would be to take your grandmother some of the beautiful flowers that bloom by the path."

That did seem to be a good idea.

It was rather late by the time that Little Red Riding Hood knocked on her granny's door.

"Come in!" called a gruff voice.

Inside the cottage, Little Red Riding Hood tiptoed toward the bed.

"Why grandmother," gasped her granddaughter, "what big ears you have!"

"The better to hear you with!" croaked the invalid.

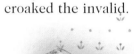

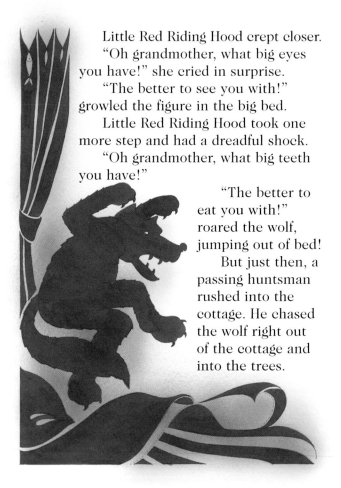

Little Red Riding Hood crept closer.

"Oh grandmother, what big eyes you have!" she cried in surprise.

"The better to see you with!" growled the figure in the big bed.

Little Red Riding Hood took one more step and had a dreadful shock.

"Oh grandmother, what big teeth you have!"

"The better to eat you with!" roared the wolf, jumping out of bed!

But just then, a passing huntsman rushed into the cottage. He chased the wolf right out of the cottage and into the trees.

Little Red Riding Hood heard a muffled sound from the cupboard. Bravely, she flung open the doors.

"Oh grandmother!" she cried with relief. "I thought you had been eaten! How are you feeling now?"

"I always feel better when I see you, Little Red Riding Hood," smiled her grandmother. "You must know that!"

THE UGLY DUCKLING

One sunny summer day, a mother duck sat on her nest.

It seemed to the duck that she had been sitting on her eggs for a long time. Then, one morning, she heard a tiny sound from one of her eggs. Out popped a fluffy duckling!

All at once, there were little sounds
from more of the eggs. Before long,
twelve fluffy little ducklings were
cuddling up to their mother.

But one of the eggs—the largest of
all—had not yet hatched. "How
annoying," said the mother duck, and
she settled down to wait a little longer.

Sure enough, a day or two later,
there was a tapping from the egg. At
last a funny little bird stood in the nest.
He was the ugliest bird she had ever
seen. He didn't look like a duckling at all.

"I'll push him into the water," said
the mother duck. "If he cannot swim,
I'll know he is a turkey."

But when she nudged the untidy bird out into the pond, he swam off quite happily. In fact, the duck felt quite proud of her ugly duckling.

She set off to introduce her children to the other animals.

In the barnyard, the other ducks and the hens quacked and clucked in approval as the mother duck led her twelve little ducklings past. But when they saw the last duckling, they shook their heads and hissed.

"What a horrible bird!" they cried.

"He will grow into his feathers," replied the mother duck. She led her brood back to the pond.

As the ducklings grew, they loved to waddle in the barnyard, shaking their feathers. But the ugly duckling soon dreaded the barnyard birds. They pecked at him and called him names.

At last a morning came when the little duckling could bear it no longer. He ran away from the barnyard.

As night fell, he came, tired and hungry, to a wild marsh. In the morning, the wild ducks who lived there found a stranger among them.

"We've never seen a duck as ugly as you!" they laughed. "But you can live here if you like." The little duckling was still lonely, but at least no one bullied him. Then one day, as he swam by the bank, he suddenly saw a dog running through the reeds. All around the marsh were hunters and their dogs.

The duckling hid in the reeds all day, trembling with fright as shots whistled over his bowed head.

That night, he fled from his unsafe home.

The weather was growing colder when he came to a cottage and crept inside to escape the coming storm.

An old woman lived there with her cat and her hen. She let the duckling stay, but the animals were not friendly.

"You are no use at all," the cat and hen said.

At last, the duckling could bear the unkindness no longer. He wandered out into the world once more.

When the duckling came to a lake,
he realized how much he had missed
swimming. But winter was coming,
and the nights grew colder.

One frosty day, a flock of beautiful
white birds flew over the lake. He did
not know that they were swans.

One morning, the poor duckling
woke to find that he had become
trapped in the frozen water. Luckily, a
passing farmer freed him and carried
him home to his family.

But the youngster was clumsy and
knocked over dishes and pots. The
farmer's wife angrily chased him from
the house.

But gradually, the days became
lighter. The bird found that his wings
were stronger, and he could fly swiftly
over the water. One afternoon, he
caught sight of the beautiful white
birds he had seen before far below.

As he landed, the swans rushed
toward him, beating their wings. The
bird bowed his head, waiting for their
attack. As he did so, he saw his
reflection. He wasn't an ugly duckling
at all! He had grown up … into a
beautiful white swan! The other swans
had come to welcome him.

"Oh look," cried some
children who had come to
feed the birds, "that new
swan is the most beautiful
one of all!"

Snow White and the Seven Dwarfs

One winter's day, a Queen sat sewing by an open window. Suddenly, she pricked her finger, and a drop of red blood fell on the snow below.

"I wish I could have a daughter with skin as white as snow, lips as red as blood, and hair as black as the window frame," sighed the Queen.

Before long, the Queen's wish came true. She called her baby Snow White, but sadly died soon after. The heartbroken King soon became lonely and found himself a new bride. She was very beautiful, but her heart was cold. Every day she looked into her mirror and asked:
"Magic mirror on the wall, Who is the fairest one of all?"

And the mirror would reply:
"O Queen, now I can truly say, You are the fairest one this day."

But the day came when the mirror
gave another reply.

"O Queen, your time has fled away,
Snow White is the fairest one today."

The Queen called for a huntsman.
"Take Snow White into the forest,"
she told him, "and bring me back her
heart to show that she is dead."

The man did as the Queen had
said, but when the moment came to
kill the girl, he could not do it.

"Just leave me here," begged Snow
White. "I promise never to come home."

So the huntsman took back an
animal's heart and left the girl behind.

Snow White wandered through the
trees for hours. Then, just when she
thought she could go no farther, she
saw a little cottage. No one came to
answer her knock, so she tiptoed inside.

What a curious little house it was!
On the table were seven little plates
and seven little glasses. Poor Snow
White was so hungry that she took a
little food. Then, she climbed up the
winding stairs to the bedroom.

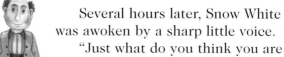

Several hours later, Snow White was awoken by a sharp little voice.

"Just what do you think you are doing in our house?" it asked.

Snow White looked up to see seven little men, in working clothes, standing around. She explained what had happened to her.

"And now," she said, "I have nowhere to go at all."

"Yes, you do!" chorused the little men. "You can stay here with us! But you must promise us never to open the door to a stranger."

So Snow White
stayed with the
little men. Her life
was very different
from the one she
had lived at home.
She longed for
someone to talk to during the long days.

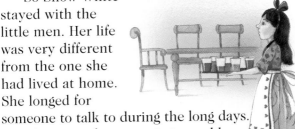

Then, one fine morning, an old
woman, with a basket of pretty things,
knocked on the cottage door.

Snow White could not resist
talking to the woman through the
open window.

Snow White did not realize that
her visitor was none other than the
wicked Queen in disguise. For months,
the Queen had been so happy that
she did not consult her mirror. When
she did, she had a terrible shock.

*"O Queen, you'll not have your will,
For Snow White is the fairest still."*

Raging through her kingdom, the
Queen had hunted high and low for
the missing girl.

"You are wise not to open the door to strangers, my dear," she smiled. "But to show that there are no hard feelings, please take this red apple as a gift from a new friend."

It seemed impolite to refuse. Snow White waved goodbye and took one bite.

When the little men returned from their work that evening, they found Snow White lying lifeless on the floor, the apple still clutched in her hand.

"This is the work of the Queen, I'm sure," cried one little man, sobbing.

Sadly, the little men took their friend and placed her in a crystal coffin.

One morning, a young Prince rode by and saw the coffin and the lovely girl inside. He fell in love with her at once.

"Let me take her back to my palace," he begged, "where she can lie in state as befits a Princess."

The little men agreed that she deserved no less. Carefully, they helped the Prince to lift the coffin. But as they did so, the piece of apple caught in Snow White's throat was dislodged. She sat up and smiled at the Prince.

Snow White and her Prince lived happily ever after. And the wicked Queen was so eaten up with rage that she died soon after.

THE SHADOW

Once there was a writer who went to live in a hot country. Opposite his home was a house that seemed to be empty. But as he sat on his balcony one night, with the lighted room behind him, the man saw that his shadow seemed to be sitting on the opposite balcony.

"If only you could go inside for me and explore that house," said the man. And, you know, when he got up and went inside, the shadow did look as though it went into the house opposite.

The next morning, the man was astonished to find that he had no shadow at all! But by the time he returned to his home far away, his shadow had grown again.

One evening, there was a knock at the door. Standing outside was a very thin man.

"I suppose you don't recognize me," said the visitor, "I am your old shadow. I have become rich and wise since I left you."

Then the Shadow described how he had entered the house opposite and found that a goddess named Poetry lived there.

"A great desire came upon me to be a man," said the Shadow, "but I had no clothes or money. The next day—don't laugh!—I hid under the baker woman's skirts and didn't come out until nighttime. Then I ran here and there, telling people truths about themselves. And they were so afraid that their friends would find out that they gave me rich presents."

Then the Shadow took his leave.

A year passed, and the Shadow called on his old master again.

"Things are going even better for me," he said. "Look, I have grown quite plump. I feel like taking a trip and I would like a companion. Will you come with me—as my shadow?"

"That's crazy," said the man. "Of course not."

But the next year, the man
became tired and ill. His friends told
him that he looked like a shadow!

When the Shadow called again,
the man agreed that a warmer climate
would be good for his health. So he set
off with the Shadow, and stayed at his
side always, as a good shadow should.

At last the Shadow and his shadow
reached a spa, where people go to get
better from illnesses. Also staying
there was a Princess. She talked to
the shadow-man, and found him very
intelligent. That made her think, "I
will marry the man who is so amazing
that even his shadow is wise."

As the wedding preparations were made, the Shadow said to the man, "Listen, I will give you money and a state coach if only you will always stay with me and never tell a soul that I was once your shadow."

"Never!" cried the man.

Then the Shadow ran quickly to the girl, looking shocked and pale.

"My shadow has gone crazy," he told her, "and thinks he is human!"

"It might be better," said the Princess, "if he was never seen again."

So that night, when the wedding took place, the Shadow's shadow was not there, and he has never been seen since.

THE TINDERBOX

One fine day, a soldier met a witch upon the road. "If you will climb into the hollow in that tree for me," she said, "you will be a rich man. All I want is an old tinderbox that you will find in there."

The soldier agreed. Inside the tree he found three chests of money, each guarded by a huge dog. He dealt with the dogs as the witch had said, filled his pockets with money, and, picking up the old tinderbox, climbed out again.

"You can cut off my head before I'll tell you why I want that old tinderbox," said the witch. So the soldier did!

After that, the soldier lived a fine life, but in a very short time, all his money was spent. Now he lived in an attic room.

One evening, the soldier felt in his pocket and found the old tinderbox. He thought he would use it to light his last candle. But as he struck three sparks from the flint, the dogs from inside the tree appeared before him. And the dogs were ready to do whatever the soldier asked, bringing him money, jewels, and other fine things.

Soon the soldier was as rich and happy as he had been before. One day, he heard of a beautiful Princess. Feeling curious, he sent the first dog to fetch her.

As soon as he saw the Princess, the soldier wanted to marry her. He kissed her and sent her home.

After that, the soldier could not help sending one of his dogs to fetch the Princess each night. But it was not long before the King and Queen tracked him down. He was quickly thrown into prison and sentenced to death.

"If only I had my tinderbox with me," said the soldier. He managed to give a message to a little boy outside his window, who ran off to fetch it.

With the tinderbox in his hand once more, the soldier knew that nothing could hurt him. He summoned the three dogs, who quickly over-powered the guards and chased away the King and Queen.

The people were happy to offer the throne to the Princess, and she was happy to accept it—and the hand of the handsome soldier whose face she had seen in her dreams.

RAPUNZEL

Once there lived a man and wife who wanted very much to have a child of their own. But year after year passed, and they did not have a baby. Often, the woman would sit sadly looking out of the window, from which she could see the garden next door.

Now this garden was very beautiful, full of flowers and vegetables, but no one dared to enter it because it belonged to a witch. One day, as the woman looked out, she suddenly had a great longing to eat one of the lettuces growing below.

She looked so pale and anxious that her husband agreed to fetch her a lettuce.

That evening, the man crept over the garden wall. He was about to cut a lettuce when a voice cackled, "How dare you steal from me?"

It was the witch! Stuttering with fright, the man explained about his wife's great craving for lettuce.

"Very well," laughed the witch. "You may take a lettuce, if you will give me your firstborn child in return."

The man was so frightened that he agreed and hurried home.

And only a few months later, his wife gave birth to a beautiful baby girl. The witch made the man keep his promise. She took the child at once and called her Rapunzel.

The little girl grew quickly and became more lovely every day. The witch treated her like her own child, but when Rapunzel was twelve years old, the witch took her to a high tower and put her in a room at the very top. There was no door and no stairs— just a small window.

When the witch visited, she called out,

*"Rapunzel,
Rapunzel,
Let down your hair!"*

At this, the girl would lower her long, braided hair from the window, and the witch would climb up.

A few years later, a Prince came riding past and heard a beautiful voice singing from the top of the tower. He hid nearby and saw what the witch did.

As soon as the witch had gone, the Prince came out of his hiding place and called out,

"*Rapunzel, Rapunzel,*
Let down your hair!"

Thinking that the witch had returned, Rapunzel did as she was asked. She was astonished to see a tall, handsome young man climbing through the high window instead.

The Prince spoke kindly to the girl and, as she grew to know him, she grew to love him.

All went well until one day, when the witch climbed into the tower, Rapunzel spoke without thinking.

"Why is it, Mother, that you feel so much heavier than the Prince does?"

The witch flew into a rage. She took out some scissors and snipped off Rapunzel's long braid. With her magic powers, she banished the frightened girl to a desert far away. Then she crouched near the window and waited.

Before long, a voice drifted up:
"Rapunzel, Rapunzel,
Let down your hair!"

It was the Prince.
Carefully, the witch
lowered the braid of
hair out of the window.
As the Prince climbed
into the room, she cried:
"I wanted to keep my
darling safe from such
as you!" And she gave
him a huge push.

The Prince fell like a stone into
some bushes at the foot of the tower.
He managed to stagger to his feet, but
his eyes had been scratched by
thorns, and he could not see at all. He
stumbled away to a life of wandering.

Years later, the Prince
came to the desert where
Rapunzel was living. He
heard her sweet
voice, singing sadly.

"Rapunzel!"
he cried,
running
forward.

The poor girl covered his face
with kisses. As her tears of joy fell onto
the Prince's eyes, he found he could
see the girl he loved.

The Prince and Rapunzel returned
to his kingdom, where they lived happily
together for the rest of their days. The
witch was never heard of again.

THE FIR TREE

Once upon a time, a little fir tree grew in a forest. All around him were beautiful trees, but the little fir tree was not happy. He wanted to be bigger.

"I wish I could be cut down," he said, "as the biggest trees are each year. Then I would travel over the sea. How wonderful!"

The little tree knew that the largest trees were made into the masts of ships. Each year at Christmas time, some smaller trees were cut down, too. "They are taken into people's homes," said the sparrows, "and decorated with toys."

That sounded even better to the little tree. He could think only of growing bigger. He cared nothing for his lovely home. All he wanted was to be grown up and gone.

And the very next Christmas, he was one of the first to be cut down.

Down in the town, the fir tree was chosen by a very grand family and carried back to their home. How proud he felt, covered with candles, ornaments, and presents.

That night, the children danced around the tree and opened their presents. It was such a pretty sight!

Next morning, some servants removed the rest of the decorations and put the tree away in a storeroom. Only the golden star on his highest branch remained.

The tree was lonely until some mice came to talk to him. They longed to hear about his life in the forest.

"I suppose I was happy," said the
fir tree. "But I did not feel it then."

Some months later, when the fir
tree was yellow and dry, he was taken
out into the yard.

The children stamped on his
branches and broke them.

Then the tree realized how
happy he had been in the
storeroom, but he had not
felt it at the time.

Before long, a
servant came. He
chopped up the tree
for firewood. The
poor tree was burned
on the kitchen stove.

"How happy I
was in the yard,"
he sighed.

Poor tree! All his
life, he had always
been wishing for
something else, and
never felt truly happy.
Don't be like him, will you?

THE TWELVE DANCING PRINCESSES

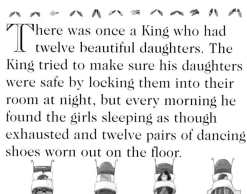

There was once a King who had twelve beautiful daughters. The King tried to make sure his daughters were safe by locking them into their room at night, but every morning he found the girls sleeping as though exhausted and twelve pairs of dancing shoes worn out on the floor.

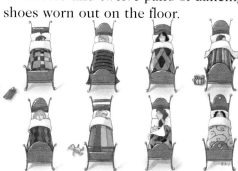

The more the King thought about it, the more worried he became. At last he made a proclamation that whoever could solve the mystery might choose one of the girls to be his wife and become heir to the throne. But if, after three nights, the suitor was no nearer to the truth, then he must lose his life.

Several Princes came to try. But they all fell asleep outside the Princesses' room. And they all lost their heads.

One day, a wounded soldier passed through the kingdom. An old woman by the side of the road asked where he was going.

Joking, the soldier replied, "Oh, I'm going to find out what happens to the Princesses, night after night!"

The old woman answered, "That is not so difficult. You must simply leave the glass of wine that is given to you in the evening, for it is drugged. Then, put on this magic cloak. It will make you invisible."

When the soldier presented himself
at the palace, he was given fine clothes
to wear and shown to his bed in the
hallway. The eldest Princess brought
him a glass of wine, but he was careful
only to pretend to drink it.

Then the soldier lay down and snored
loudly to show that he was asleep.

As soon as they heard his snores,
the Princesses put on brand new
dancing shoes and their finest clothes.

Then the eldest Princess went to the head of her bed and pressed a secret panel. A passageway opened up behind it. One by one, the Princesses went through.

Quickly, the soldier threw on the magic cloak and went after the girls.

But in his hurry, as he followed them down the stairs, he stepped on the youngest Princess's dress.

"What was that?" she cried.

"Don't be silly," the oldest Princess replied. "Come on!"

Before long, the Princesses reached
the bottom of the stairs and came to
an avenue of trees with leaves of silver
and gold, gleaming in the moonlight.

The soldier broke a twig from the
nearest tree.

"What was that?" The youngest
Princess heard the tiny sound.

But the eldest Princess told her to
be quiet.

"Hurry along," she said.

Next the Princesses came to an avenue of trees with diamond leaves. Once again, the soldier broke off a twig as evidence.

"I heard something again, I'm sure of it," whispered the youngest Princess. But once more her sister silenced her.

At last they came to a lake where twelve boats and twelve Princes were waiting. The Princesses climbed in, and the soldier joined the boat of the youngest Princess, but of course, she and her partner could not see him.

Across the lake stood
a fine castle. From its
open doors the sound
of music streamed
out over the water.
Laughing and
talking, the Princesses
and their Princes
hurried inside, where
they were soon swept away by the
waves of music.

By three o'clock in the morning, the Princesses' shoes were worn out. Saying goodbye to their Princes, they hurried back to their room in the palace.

This time, the soldier made sure he went ahead of them.

For two more nights, the soldier followed the Princesses. On the third night, he brought back a golden goblet.

"I have found the answer to the mystery," the soldier told the King, and he related everything that had happened to the dancing Princesses.

"And here," he said, producing the twigs and the goblet, "is my proof."

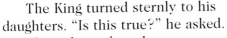

The King turned sternly to his daughters. "Is this true?" he asked.

The girls confessed at once.

"Then you may choose whichever one of these troublesome girls you would like for your bride," the King told the soldier.

"I am not so young myself," the suitor laughed. "I will choose the eldest, who was so certain that there was no one following. But I am sure that all of her sisters will gladly dance at our wedding!"

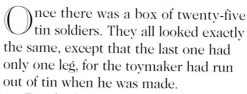

THE BRAVE TIN SOLDIER

Once there was a box of twenty-five tin soldiers. They all looked exactly the same, except that the last one had only one leg, for the toymaker had run out of tin when he was made.

But the last tin soldier was just as brave as his brothers. At night, when the toys jumped up and played by themselves, he looked around and saw a fine toy castle with a lady at the door. She was very pretty, and she only had one leg, too!

"She would make a fine wife for me," said the tin soldier.

In fact, the pretty lady was a dancer, standing on one leg. Her other leg was tucked under her skirts.

Now the soldier was sitting on a jack-in-the-box! At midnight, the box burst open, and the soldier went flying over to the windowsill.

Next morning, when the windows were opened, he fell out! He landed on the pavement. Although his owner came to look for him, he went sadly back indoors when it started to rain.

When the rain ended, two boys saw the toy soldier and decided to put him in a paper boat.

At first all was well. The soldier stood up straight and strong, and the boat sailed off along the water running along the street. Then the water rushed into a drain, and the soldier found himself whirling into a dark cave.

"Halt! Who goes there?" cried a big water rat. The soldier, having no choice, rushed on.

Before he could do anything, the soldier's boat sank, leaving him floundering. Just at that moment, a passing fish opened its jaws and swallowed him!

Strangely enough,
the fish was caught
and taken to market.
It was bought by the
cook from the soldier's
old home! In no time
at all, he found himself
back in the nursery.

The tin soldier
looked longingly at the
lady in the castle, and she
looked longingly at him. But the soldier's
adventures were not over. A little boy
threw him into the fire. The little man
stood and felt himself melting. At that
moment, a rush of air sent the pretty
lady flying into the fire to join him.

Next morning, when he raked out
the fire, a servant found a tin heart—
all that was left of the brave soldier
and his lady love.